William Kotzwinkle, Glenn Murray, and Elizabeth Gundy

Walter the Farting Dog
Banned from the Beach

Illustrated by **Audrey Colman**

PUFFIN BOOKS

PUFFIN BOOKS
Published by the Penguin Group
Penguin Young Readers Group, 345 Hudson Street, New York, New York 10014, U.S.A.
Penguin Group (Canada), 90 Eglinton Avenue East, Suite 700, Toronto, Ontario, Canada M4P 2Y3
(a division of Pearson Penguin Canada Inc.)
Penguin Books Ltd, 80 Strand, London WC2R ORL, England
Penguin Ireland, 25 St Stephen's Green, Dublin 2, Ireland (a division of Penguin Books Ltd)
Penguin Group (Australia), 250 Camberwell Road, Camberwell, Victoria 3124, Australia
(a division of Pearson Australia Group Pty Ltd)
Penguin Books India Pvt Ltd, 11 Community Centre, Panchsheel Park, New Delhi - 110 017, India
Penguin Group (NZ), 67 Apollo Drive, Rosedale, North Shore 0632, New Zealand
(a division of Pearson New Zealand Ltd)
Penguin Books (South Africa) (Pty) Ltd, 24 Sturdee Avenue, Rosebank, Johannesburg 2196, South Africa

Registered Offices: Penguin Books Ltd, 80 Strand, London WC2R ORL, England

First published in the United States of America by Dutton Children's Books,
a division of Penguin Young Readers Group, 2007
Published by Puffin Books, a division of Penguin Young Readers Group, 2009

22 23 24 25 26 27 28 29 30

Text copyright © William Kotzwinkle, Glenn Murray, and Elizabeth Gundy, 2007
Illustrations copyright © Audrey Colman, 2007
All rights reserved

CIP Data is available.
ISBN: 978-0-525-47812-6 (hc)

Puffin Books ISBN 978-0-14-241394-4

Manufactured in China

Designed by Jason Henry

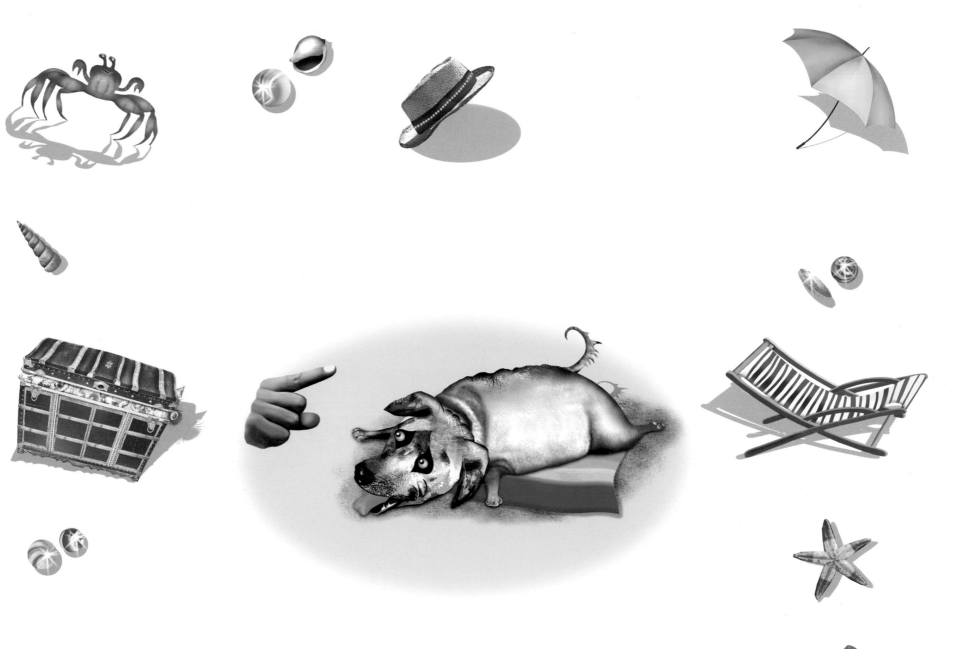

For everyone who's ever felt
misjudged or misunderstood

Mr. and Mrs. Crabbe were having a ton of fun. There was sand and sea and sunshine every day. There was swimming and snorkeling and parasailing and lots of staff to boss around.

"You there!" called Mrs. Crabbe to the pool attendant. "Get that leaf out of the water."

"And bring us some fresh towels," said Mr. Crabbe. "Make it snappy."

"If only that dog weren't ruining my view," said Mrs. Crabbe.

The dog was Walter, digging happily in the sand. You never know where an old bone might be hiding.

He detected something under the sand and dug more frantically. *Treasure! A bone, and it's a big one!* He strained to tug it free, and let out an enormous fart.

The umbrella that was shading Mr. and Mrs. Crabbe was blown into the sea. They watched aghast as it was carried away by the undertow.

At that moment, Father and Mother arrived with Betty and Billy. Mr. Crabbe stomped over to Father. "Is this your dog?"

"Yes," admitted Father. "That's our Walter."

"He shouldn't be allowed on the beach," shouted Mr. Crabbe. "He blew away our umbrella."

"It couldn't have been Walter. It was probably the sea breeze."

"The sea breeze doesn't smell like that!" said Mrs. Crabbe.

That evening, Mother said, "Wouldn't it be wonderful if we had our own little vacation home right on the beach?"

"We can't afford it," said Father, who'd just bought himself a new set of golf clubs. "Walter eats us out of house and home."

Walter farted guiltily.

There was a knock on the door. It was the manager of the resort. "We've been getting complaints about that dog of yours. We can't allow him on the beach."

"I didn't see any rule against dogs in your brochure," said Father.

"It's a new rule, and it starts today." The manager stomped off.

"Sorry, Walter," said Father. "You're banned from the beach."

Walter farted sadly.

"Never mind, Walter," said Billy. "Let's go for a walk in the village."

"Just stay away from the beach," warned Mother.

In the quaint little village, lights twinkled in the trees. Everyone was enjoying the gentle breeze and the sweet smells of the tropical night.

Walter was enjoying himself, too. *Travel broadens a dog's mind,* he thought, farting philosophically.

The Crabbes were sitting nearby at a sidewalk café, complaining about their Key lime pie. Mrs. Crabbe counted the problems on her fingers. "It's not big enough. It's not green enough. It's not sweet enough."

"Or maybe it's *too* sweet," said Mr. Crabbe, smacking his lips.

A pelican flapped its wings at Walter, and Walter farted in alarm. The power of Walter's fart blew the meringue off Mr. Crabbe's pie. It landed in his face and made an awful mess.

The Crabbes glared at Walter. "That dog is ruining our vacation."

Next morning, Father got a phone call from the chief of police.

"I've had serious complaints about your dog," said the chief. "I'm afraid we can't allow him on our streets."

Father hung up. "Sorry, Walter. You're banned from the village."

"But where can Walter go now?" asked Billy.

"He's grounded," said Father. "He stays inside."

"That's not a very nice vacation for Walter," said Betty.

Walter farted.

"Need I say more?" asked Father.

When everyone went out to have fun, Walter stayed inside with his nose pressed against the window.

Well, thought Walter, *I'll just have to make the best of it.*

He sniffed around for something to eat and found a sack of strange-looking tropical fruit. The label said COOK THOROUGHLY. DO NOT EAT RAW! Since Walter couldn't read, he ate it anyway.

Then he went to snooze in the sunshine pouring through the window.

Betty and Billy were building a sandcastle on the beach.

"Look," said Betty, pointing out to sea. "How did that island get there? It wasn't there before."

"It must've been underwater," said Billy. "Now that the tide is out, we can get there. Let's go!"

They waded out through the shallow water to explore the mysterious island.

"This is the sort of place where you find buried treasure," said Billy, beginning to dig.

Suddenly something shiny glittered in the sunlight.

"I knew it!" yelled Billy, holding up a nickel.

"We're rich!" yelled Betty.

Mr. Crabbe sat up under his new beach umbrella. "Those nasty children seem to have found something."

The Crabbes waded out to the little island.

"Let me help you," said Mr. Crabbe, pushing Billy aside.

Mr. Crabbe found a rusty old key and waved it triumphantly. "I have a feeling that this will unlock something very important," he said. Sure enough, ten minutes later, he dug up a door, and the key fit perfectly.

"Maybe we'll find a whole vacation house!" said Betty.

Though they dug for hours, they didn't find anything else, and they didn't notice that their island was shrinking. The tide was rising fast, and the waves began to lap at their feet.

Betty looked up and gasped. "How did the beach get so far away?"

"It's the tide," cried Billy. "We're marooned."

"Out of my way!" shouted Mr. Crabbe and leaped into the water. Mrs. Crabbe dove in after him, followed by Betty and Billy.

They swam as hard as they could, but the undertow was too strong. The current swirled them around and dumped them back on their shrinking little island.

"Our only hope is to build a raft," said Mr. Crabbe.

Walter woke from his nap with a bad feeling. *Betty and Billy must be in trouble!*

Walter's stomach was rumbling like a volcano from the tropical fruit that should have been thoroughly cooked, but he ignored it and raced to the screen door.

Locked!

He stepped back and charged, bursting through the screen and leaving a Walter-shaped hole in the door.

Walter ran to the beach and saw four figures in the distance with the water rising around them. Mr. and Mrs. Crabbe were launching their raft. Billy was trying to help Betty. All Walter could see of Betty was her little head above the surface and her arms waving frantically.

Walter plunged into the surf. Shooting pains twisted him around and flung him back onto the beach.

Was it a cramp from swimming too soon after eating?

No, it was the tropical fruit that should have been thoroughly cooked.

"Walter, save us!" cried Billy.

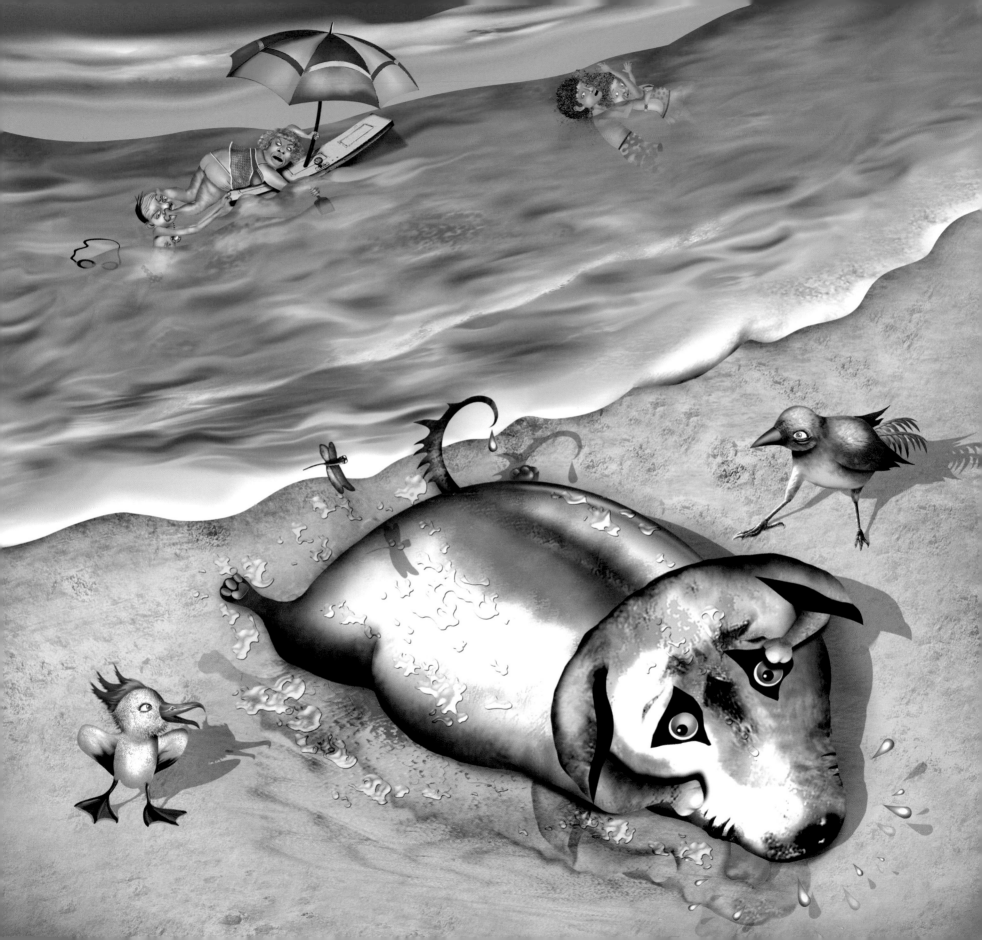

Walter struggled to rise, but the gases produced by the tropical fruit that should have been thoroughly cooked chose this moment to erupt with terrible force. The tropical-fruit fart produced a boom that was heard along the coast for miles. Coconuts blew off the trees, and the Crabbes, clutching

their new umbrella, were blown all the way to the Sandwich Islands.

The waves parted around the little island where Betty and Billy were stranded. Layer upon layer of sand and shells were pushed aside, leaving a pathway across the ocean floor.

Betty and Billy ran toward shore. Halfway there, Billy tripped on something jutting from the ocean floor. Walter raced out to help him.

"It's a treasure chest," cried Billy.

Bones, thought Walter, and grabbed a handle in his teeth. He dragged the chest to the beach. Betty and Billy pried it open.

Walter was disappointed to see that it only contained jewels and gold.

With the money from the treasure, Mother and Father
bought the vacation home of their dreams. There was sunshine
every day. There was golf and snorkeling and parasailing on the
gentle sea breezes.

Experts said it was the most important treasure uncovered
in a century. But Betty and Billy disagreed.

"Walter," they said, "you're the greatest treasure of all."